This book belongs to

Franklin's Classic Treasury

Franklin

Franklin is a trademark of Kids Can Press Ltd.

Franklin's Classic Treasury
© 1999 Contextx Inc. and Brenda Clark Illustrator Inc.

This book includes the following stories:
Franklin in the Dark first published in 1986
Hurry Up, Franklin first published in 1989
Franklin Fibs first published in 1991
Franklin is Bossy first published in 1993

All text © 1986, 1989, 1991, 1993 Contextx Inc.
All illustrations © 1986, 1989, 1991, 1993
Brenda Clark Illustrator Inc.

Kids Can Press acknowledges the financial support of the Ontario Arts Council, the Canada Council for the Arts and the Government of Canada, through the BPIDP, for our publishing activity.

Published in Canada by
Kids Can Press Ltd.
29 Birch Avenue
Toronto, ON M4V 1E2

Published in the U.S. by
Kids Can Press Ltd.
2250 Military Road
Tonawanda, NY 14150

www.kidscanpress.com

Printed in Hong Kong, China, by Wing King Tong Co. Ltd.

This book is smyth sewn casebound.

CM 99 0 9 8 7 6 5

Canadian Cataloguing in Publication Data

Bourgeois, Paulette
    Franklin's classic treasury

Contents: [v. 1] Franklin in the dark – [v. 2] Hurry up Franklin –
[v. 3] Franklin fibs – [v. 4] Franklin is bossy.

ISBN 1-55074-742-8

I. Clark, Brenda. II. Title.

PS8553.O85477F85   1999   jC813'.54   C99-930503-4
PZ7.B6654Fr 1999

Kids Can Press is a *Corus*™ Entertainment company

❇ Franklin's ❇
CLASSIC
Treasury

Paulette Bourgeois • Brenda Clark

Kids Can Press

Contents

Franklin in the Dark

Written by Paulette Bourgeois
Illustrated by Brenda Clark

FRANKLIN could slide down a riverbank all by himself. He could count forwards and backwards. He could even zip zippers and button buttons. But Franklin was afraid of small, dark places and that was a problem because…

Franklin was a turtle. He was afraid of crawling into his small, dark shell. And so, Franklin the turtle dragged his shell behind him.

Every night, Franklin's mother would take a flashlight and shine it into his shell.

"See," she would say, "there's nothing to be afraid of."

She always said that. She wasn't afraid of anything. But Franklin was sure that creepy things, slippery things, and monsters lived inside his small, dark shell.

So Franklin went looking for help. He walked until he met a duck.

"Excuse me, Duck. I'm afraid of small, dark places and I can't crawl inside my shell. Can you help me?"

"Maybe," quacked the duck. "You see, I'm afraid of very deep water. Sometimes, when nobody is watching, I wear my water wings. Would my water wings help you?"

"No," said Franklin. "I'm not afraid of water."

So Franklin walked and walked until he met a lion.

"Excuse me, Lion. I'm afraid of small, dark places and I can't crawl inside my shell. Can you help me?"

"Maybe," roared the lion. "You see, I'm afraid of great, loud noises. Sometimes, when nobody is looking, I wear my earmuffs. Would my earmuffs help you?"

"No," said Franklin. "I'm not afraid of great, loud noises."

So Franklin walked and walked and walked until he met a bird.

"Excuse me, Bird. I'm afraid of small, dark places and I can't crawl inside my shell. Can you help me?"

"Maybe," chirped the bird. "I'm afraid of flying so high that I get dizzy and fall to the ground. Sometimes, when nobody is looking, I pull my parachute. Would my parachute help you?"

"No," said Franklin. "I'm not afraid of flying high and getting dizzy."

So Franklin walked and walked and walked and walked until he met a polar bear.

"Excuse me, Polar Bear. I'm afraid of small, dark places and I can't crawl inside my shell. Can you help me?"

"Maybe," growled the bear. "You see, I'm afraid of freezing on icy, cold nights. Sometimes, when nobody is looking, I wear my snowsuit to bed. Would my snowsuit help you?"

"No," said Franklin. "I'm not afraid of freezing on icy, cold nights."

Franklin was tired and hungry. He walked and walked and walked until he met his mother.

"Oh, Franklin. I was so afraid you were lost."

"You were afraid? I didn't know mothers were ever afraid," said Franklin.

"Well, did you find some help?" she asked.
"No. I met a duck who was afraid of deep
water."
"Hmmm," she said.

"Then I met a lion who was afraid of great, loud noises."

"Uh, hmmmm," she said.

"And then I met a bird who was afraid of
falling and a polar bear who was afraid of freezing."
"Oh," she said. "They were all afraid of
something."
"Hmmmm," said Franklin.

It was getting late. Franklin was very tired and very hungry. They walked and walked until they were home.

Franklin's mother gave him a cold supper and
a warm hug. And then she sent him off to bed.
"Goodnight, dear," she said.

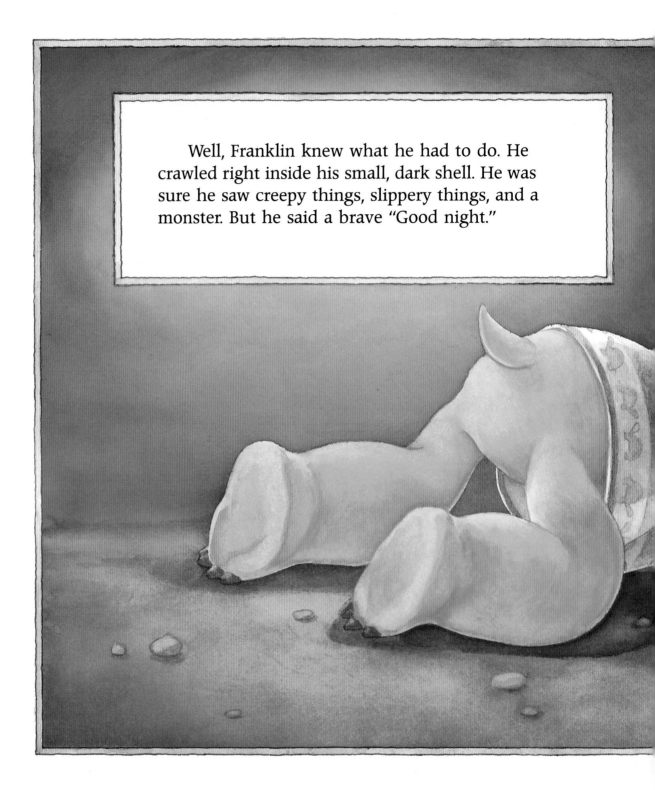

Well, Franklin knew what he had to do. He crawled right inside his small, dark shell. He was sure he saw creepy things, slippery things, and a monster. But he said a brave "Good night."

And then, when nobody was looking, Franklin the turtle turned on his night light.

Hurry Up, Franklin

Written by Paulette Bourgeois
Illustrated by Brenda Clark

FRANKLIN could slide down a river bank all by himself. He could count forwards and backwards. He could zip zippers and button buttons. He could even sleep alone in his small, dark shell. But Franklin was slow…

Even for a turtle.

"Hurry up, Franklin," pleaded his mother.
"Hurry up, Franklin," begged his father. "Hurry up,
Franklin," shouted his friends.

"I'll be there in a minute," said Franklin. But
there was always so much to see and so much to
do. Franklin was never there in just a minute.

One day Franklin was very excited. He was going to Bear's house. It was a special day. A very special day. "Hurry up," said Franklin's mother. "You can't be late."

It wasn't far to Bear's house. Just along the
path, over the bridge and across the berry patch.
Franklin meant to hurry–except he saw something
unusual. He wandered off the path and found
Rabbit bobbing up and down in the tall, green
grass.

"What are you doing?" Franklin asked Rabbit.

"Playing Leap Frog," said Rabbit. "Do you
want to play with me?"

"I'm on my way to Bear's house," said Franklin.
"And I can't be late."

"There's lots of time," said Rabbit, forgetting
that Franklin was slow, even for a turtle. "It's just
along the path, over the bridge and across the
berry patch. Come and play with me."

Franklin knew it wasn't far and so he said yes. Rabbit leaped over Franklin again and again. But after a while Rabbit said, "It's time to go. Hurry up, Franklin, or you'll be late." Then Rabbit bounded along the path on his way to Bear's house.

"I'll be there in a minute," said Franklin. And he meant to be there in just a minute – except he heard an odd sound. Franklin wandered even farther off the path until he found Otter sliding up and down the river bank.

"What are you doing?" Franklin asked Otter.

"Slipping and sliding," answered Otter. "Do you want to play with me?"

"I'm on my way to Bear's house," said Franklin. "And I can't be late."

"There's lots of time," said Otter, forgetting that Franklin was slow, even for a turtle. "It's just along the path, over the bridge and across the berry patch. Come and play with me."

Franklin knew it wasn't far and so he said yes. Franklin slid down the river bank and splashed and blew bubbles until Otter said, "It's time to go. Hurry up, Franklin, or you'll be late." Then Otter swam away with a flick of her tail on her way to Bear's house.

"I'll be there in a minute," said Franklin.

It was very quiet. Franklin was alone and far from the path. Rabbit had gone. Otter had gone. Franklin had a frightening thought. Maybe he was already too late!

Franklin walked as fast as his turtle legs could walk. He hurried through the fields and along the path. He was almost at the bridge when he heard a rustle in the grass and saw a patch of reddish fur. It was Fox, hiding in the brush.

"Do you want to play with me?" asked Fox.

"I have to hurry," said Franklin. "I'm on my way to Bear's house!"

"It's not very far," said Fox. "Just over the bridge and across the berry patch. Come and play hide and seek."

Franklin hesitated. Hide and seek was his favourite game.

"Ready or not?" asked Fox.

Franklin shouted, "Ready!" And he was just about to step off the path when he remembered it was a very special day and he couldn't be late.

"I can't play," said Franklin. "I have to hurry."

Franklin rushed along the path and over the bridge. He was in such a hurry that he almost stepped on Snail.

"Where are you going in such a hurry?" asked Snail, who was even slower than Franklin.

"I'm on my way to Bear's house," said Franklin. "I have to hurry. I can't be late. Being late would ruin everything."

Snail began to cry.

"What's wrong?" asked Franklin.

"I'll never get to Bear's house on time," sobbed Snail.

"It's not very far," said Franklin. "Just across the berry patch."

It seemed very far to Snail, and he sobbed even harder.

"Don't worry," said Franklin bravely. But even Franklin was worried. It was farther than he thought. It was a very big berry patch. He wished he hadn't played with Rabbit. He wished he hadn't played with Otter. He wished he hadn't wasted so much time talking to Fox. Then he remembered it was Bear's special day. There was no time to cry. He had to hurry.

"Come along, Snail," said Franklin, helping Snail slide onto his back.

"Please hurry," whispered Snail. But Franklin needed no urging. He moved surely and steadily. He hurried past the blackberries. He hurried past the gooseberries. He even hurried past the raspberries. And he was almost at Bear's front gate when he remembered something important.

He stopped right there at the edge of the berry patch and started picking handfuls of the ripest, plumpest, juiciest blueberries in the berry patch.

"We don't have time to pick berries," said Snail. "You know we can't be late."

Franklin whispered into Snail's right ear. And soon Snail was helping too. They picked until the bush was clean.

"Hurry up," said Snail. "Please hurry up, Franklin."

He hurried up Bear's path, through the front door, across the kitchen and into Bear's living room.

Rabbit was there. Otter was there. Fox was there. Everyone was there. Franklin and Snail had made it just in time to shout:

"Surprise! Have a Happy Birthday, Bear!"

And he did.

Franklin Fibs

Written by Paulette Bourgeois
Illustrated by Brenda Clark

FRANKLIN could slide down a riverbank all by himself. He could count forwards and backwards. He could zip zippers and button buttons. He could even tie shoe laces, but Franklin could not swallow seventy-six flies in the blink of an eye.

And that was a problem because Franklin said he could. He told all his friends he could. Franklin had fibbed.

It started with Bear.
Bear boasted, "I can climb the highest tree."
He scrambled to the tip of a pine.

Then Hawk bragged, "I can fly over the berry patch without flapping my wings."

He soared over the woods and past the berry patch without ruffling a feather.

Beaver crowed, "I can chop down a tree with just my teeth."

Beaver gnawed first on one side, then on the other. Chips of wood flew this way and that. The tree crashed down.

"And," she said, "I can make my own dam."

Franklin couldn't climb a tree. He couldn't chop down a tree. He couldn't fly. And he forgot everything he *could* do. So he fibbed.

"I can swallow seventy-six flies in the blink of an eye," he said.

His friends were astounded.

"Watch me," said Franklin.

Franklin gobbled two, four, six flies.

"There!"

"But that was only six flies," said Hawk.

"There were only six flies flying," said Franklin. "And I ate them all in the blink of an eye. I could have eaten seventy more."

"Let's see," said Beaver.

Franklin frowned. There was no way he could eat seventy-six flies in the blink of an eye. No way at all.

Franklin had no appetite at dinner.
"What's wrong?" asked his mother.
"I can't eat seventy-six flies in the blink of an eye."
"Neither can I," said Franklin's father.
"Neither can I," said Franklin's mother.
"But you don't have to," said Franklin sadly.

"And I do." Franklin told them all about the flies. His mother nodded and his father hmmmmed. "You have quite an imagination," said Franklin's father.

The next morning, Franklin's friends were waiting.
Beaver had a surprise.

"Eat them," she dared.

Franklin wrapped a woolly winter scarf twice around
his neck. "Can't," he squawked. "I have a sore throat."

His friends laughed.

Franklin felt terrible. He couldn't eat. He couldn't
sleep. He couldn't think of anything but flies and lies.
"I could practise until I *could* swallow seventy-six
flies in the blink of an eye," Franklin told his father.
"You could, but it would take a long time," he said.

"I could stop playing with my friends," Franklin told his mother.

"You could, but you might be lonely," she said.

"I could tell them I fibbed," said Franklin.

"You could do that," said Franklin's parents. "And then you can show them what you *can* do."

The next day, Franklin's friends were waiting.

"I can't eat seventy-six flies in the blink of an eye," admitted Franklin.

"We guessed," said Bear.

"But," said Franklin, "I *can* eat seventy-six flies."

Franklin's friends sighed.

"Really," said Franklin.

Franklin ran home.

He got the flies, a bowl, some flour, milk, eggs and honey. He poured and stirred, rolled and baked. Finally, he was ready.

94

"Watch me!" Franklin gobbled the entire fly pie.

"There," said Franklin licking his lips.

"Amazing! What else can you do?" asked Beaver.

Franklin swaggered with success. He was about to say that he could eat two fly pies in a gulp.

Then he thought twice and said nothing at all.
Even a turtle gets tired of eating fly pie.

Franklin Is Bossy

Written by Paulette Bourgeois
Illustrated by Brenda Clark

FRANKLIN the turtle could zip zippers and button buttons. He could count by twos and tie his shoes. He had lots of friends and one best friend, named Bear. They played tag and marbles, hopscotch and ball. But one day something awful happened. Franklin and Bear had a fight.

It was a steamy summer morning. Franklin told his friends, "Let's play marbles." And they did.

After a while, Franklin said, "I'm tired of marbles, let's have a race."

"You always pick the games," grumbled Bear.
Franklin paid no attention.
They started to run. Bear was in the lead.
Goose followed close behind. Franklin saw that he
was losing and cried out …

"Slowest one wins!" as he crawled across the finish line last.

"That's not fair," said Bear.

Franklin ignored him. "I'm tired of running, let's play baseball."

Bear did not put on his mitt. He did not put on his cap. He was mad.

"It's too hot. I don't want to play," said Bear.

"Me neither," said Beaver.

"It's not too hot!" said Franklin.

"Is too," said Bear.

"Is not," said Franklin.

"I don't want to play with you, Franklin!" shouted Bear.

"And I don't want to play with you, either!" Franklin shouted back.

Franklin stomped all the way home.

"What's wrong?" asked his father.

"There's no one to play with," answered Franklin.

"Maybe your friends will come by later," said Franklin's father.

"Maybe," he said.

In his room, Franklin built a castle. He made a cape to be brave in. He made shields and swords and suits of armour. He drew pictures. He played house. He read stories. He played by himself for one whole hour, and then he didn't know what to do.

So, Franklin went looking for company.
His friends were in the river, cooling off.
"Are you still hot?" he asked.
"No," they answered.
"Then let's play ball," said Franklin.

Before anyone had a chance to say a word, Franklin started giving orders. "Bear, you play first base. Goose and Beaver, you go to the outfield. I'll be the pitcher."

"No way!" shouted Bear. "I don't want to play with you. You are too bossy."

All of Franklin's friends nodded.

"Bear's right," they said.

Franklin turned his back and went home.

There was no one to play with and nothing much to do. So, he helped his father all afternoon. They weeded the garden and washed the floors. And they made supper for Mole because he was sick.

"You're a good friend," Mole told Franklin's father.

On the way home, Franklin asked, "Do you and Mole have fights?"

"Sometimes," said Franklin's father. "But we always make up."

Franklin played alone for another whole day. He missed Bear and all his friends. And he had lots of time to think.

He would go to Bear and apologize.

Franklin and Bear met on the bridge.

"I was going to your house," said Franklin.
"And I was going to your house," said Bear.
"I'm sorry," said Franklin. "It was all my fault."
"No, it was my fault," said Bear.
"Mine," said Franklin.
"No, mine," said Bear.

122

"STOP!" shouted Beaver, who was listening under the bridge.

"This is silly!" Beaver slapped her tail so hard that Franklin and Bear jumped. They started to giggle.

"Friends?" asked Franklin.
"Friends," said Bear.

Beaver wanted to play baseball. Bear and Goose and Duck agreed. They were picking teams when Franklin insisted on being the pitcher ... again.

All together his friends shouted, "No fair, Franklin!"

Franklin knew they were right. He couldn't always be pitcher. It was his turn to play in the outfield.

And it wasn't so bad, for although Franklin
didn't catch a single ball ... he did catch lots of flies.